DONATED
MR. ROBERT J.

OCT 2 6 2000

IMMANUEL LUTHERAN SCHOOL
SCHOEN MEMORIAL LIBRARY

Pirate's Promise

DONATED BY
MD. ROBERT A. KUB

Pirate's Promise

Clyde Robert Bulla

Illustrated by PETER BURCHARD

HarperTrophy
A Division of HarperCollins*Publishers*

Pirate's Promise
Copyright © 1958 by Clyde Robert Bulla
Copyright renewed 1986 by Clyde Robert Bulla
All rights reserved.
No part of this book may be used or reproduced in any manner whatsoever
without written permission except in the case of brief quotations embodied in
critical articles and reviews.
Printed in the United States of America.
For information address HarperCollins Children's Books, a division of
HarperCollins Publishers, 10 East 53rd Street, New York, NY 10022.
LC Number 58-8209
ISBN 0-06-440457-9 (pbk.)
First Harper Trophy edition, 1994.

To Mildred Phipps,

who started Tom on his long journey

Contents

1 · Big John

Late in the year 1716 Big John Ludd came home from sea. He left ship in London, but he stayed in the great city not at all. With his sea chest on his shoulder, he began to walk.

All day he walked through wind and snow. It was night when he came to a village on the bank of a river.

He stopped at a poor little house. "Open!" he shouted, and he beat on the door with his fist.

1

A cry came from inside. "Children, it's your father! Your father's come home!"

A woman opened the door. "Oh, my dear husband!" she cried.

"Let me in, woman. It's freezing cold outside." He pushed her out of the doorway and went into the house.

A few coals burned in the fireplace. There was no other light in the room.

He sat down by the fire.

"My dear husband," the woman said again. "It's good to see you there in your old place."

"How are the children?" he asked.

"As well as can be, all seven of them," she said. "They just had their supper."

"Well, where are they?" he shouted. "Don't they know their father's home?"

In the dark corners of the room, shadows began to move. A snub-nosed boy came out into the firelight. He pushed his long black hair out of his eyes.

"That's a good boy, Jacky," said the woman. "Run and give your father a kiss."

The boy's face turned red. "Oh, Ma!" he said.

"You're a fine lad, Jacky—a fine, big lad," said his father. "Now let's have a look at the others."

One by one, the rest of the seven came out into the light. They were all boys, with black hair and snub noses. The two smallest ones began to cry.

"Don't be making faces at me!" said Big John. "I'm your *father.*"

"They are only babies," said their mother, "and you've been gone a year. You can't blame them if they don't know you yet."

Jacky went close to his father. "There's more here that you've not seen," he said.

"Hush!" said his mother.

"What's this?" asked Big John. "Who is here that I've not seen?"

"Don't be angry," said his wife. "Promise me you won't be angry."

"I'll promise nothing. What are you keeping from me?" Big John tried to look into the shadows. "Who is hiding there?"

A girl came out into the light. She was a pretty girl with a pale, frightened face.

Behind her came a boy. He was straight and tall, and his hair was red. He said in a clear voice, "We weren't hiding, sir."

Big John's mouth fell open. "Well!" he said. "And who might you be?"

"Tom Pippin, sir," said the boy, "and this is my sister, Dinah."

Big John looked at his wife.

"These are my brother's children," she said. "They came here after my poor brother died. They had no mother or father—"

"They came here to *live?*" said Big John.

"They had no other place to go," she said.

"How long have they been here?" he asked.

"Two months," she said.

Jacky spoke up. "It's *three* months."

His mother said quickly, "To bed, you children. To bed now, all of you."

The children went to bed. They curled up like cats

wherever they could find a place. Some slept on an old mat. Some slept on the bare floor.

Big John and his wife sat alone by the fire.

She said in a low voice, "Don't be angry, please. I couldn't turn my brother's children away. Tom is only twelve, just the age of our Jacky. The girl is ten and small for her age. They can't look out for themselves."

"Three months!" said Big John. "Three months those brats have been here, taking the bread from my children's mouths."

"They don't eat much," she said. "The girl eats no more than a bird, and she's a good little thing. I'm glad to have a girl in the house. She helps in ever so many ways."

"That may be," said Big John, "but what about the boy?"

"Tom's not a bad boy," she said. "He and the girl are different from our children, but I'm fond of them—"

"Different?" said Big John. "How do you mean?"

"Their father was a schoolmaster, you know," she said. "They can read and write."

"They can, can they?" said Big John. "Maybe they think that makes them better than us. But they're not too good to live in my house and eat my bread."

"Please!" whispered his wife. "They'll hear you."

"Let them hear me, then," he said. "This is their last night under my roof. Out they go tomorrow!"

2 · Tom and Dinah

In the morning Big John had breakfast with his wife and children. They ate by the fire.

Tom and Dinah ate in the pantry, among the pots and pans. It was cold there, but they were glad to be alone together. They talked in whispers.

"Did you hear him last night?" asked Dinah. " 'Out they go tomorrow.' That's what he said."

"I heard him," said Tom.

"What are we going to do?" she asked.

"Sleep under the trees," he said. "Eat strawberries and cream."

"In the winter? That's foolish!" she said.

"I was only trying to make you laugh," he said. "Remember how we used to laugh and be foolish together?"

"There's nothing to laugh about in this house," she said. "Do you know it's three days till Christmas? And I've nothing to give you."

"I've nothing to give you, either," he said, "but some day I'll give you a hundred presents all at once."

The door opened. Jacky put his head into the pantry. "I hear you out there," he said. "I hear you whispering your secrets."

Tom and Dinah said nothing.

"Ma was easy on you," said Jacky, "but it won't be the same now that Pa is home. Pa doesn't like any beggars around."

"We're not beggars," said Tom.

"You will be, when Pa turns you out of the house,"

said Jacky. "Down the road you'll go, like two bobtailed birds. The wind will be blowing and the snow will be flying, and how will you like that?"

He shut the pantry door. In a moment he was back. "Pa wants to see you now."

Tom and Dinah looked at each other. Without a word they got up and followed Jacky.

Big John sat by the fire. He said to Dinah, "My wife says you help her with the work here."

"Yes, sir," she said.

"My wife says you're a good girl," he said.

"I try to be, sir," she said.

"She says she needs a girl." Big John looked at Tom. "But seven boys is enough."

"Yes, sir," said Tom.

"Did your father leave you any money?" asked Big John.

"No, sir," said Tom.

"You look able to work," said Big John. "I've got friends in London. One of them might have work for a boy your size. How does that sound to you?"

"Very good, sir," said Tom. "What kind of work would it be?"

"I couldn't say," said Big John. "I'd have to talk that over with my friends. One of these days I'll take you down to London, and we'll see what we can do."

Tom was too surprised to answer.

Afterward, when he and Dinah were alone in the pantry, he said, "Did you hear Uncle John? He's not going to turn us out. He's going to be kind to us."

"If he takes you to London, I want to go, too," said Dinah. "I want us to be together."

"So do I," said Tom. "When I get work in London,

we *will* be together. First we'll have a room or two. Then, when I get ahead in my work, we'll have a whole house."

"With a little garden?" she asked.

"We'll have a big garden if you want it," he said.

"I hope we can have a garden like the one at home," she said, "and I can sit there in summer and watch the moon come up. Tom, what made Uncle John change?" she asked. "Last night he was going to turn us out."

"Maybe he was cold and tired last night," said Tom. "Maybe he feels better today. Did you see him, Dinah? He even smiled at us."

"I saw him, and I didn't like it. It wasn't a *good* smile." Tears came to Dinah's eyes. "I wish he wouldn't take you away."

"Maybe he won't," said Tom. "He may forget all about it."

But Big John did not forget.

The next day he said to Tom, "Be ready in the morning. If tomorrow is a fine day, I'll take you down to London."

3 · Down to London

The next day was fair. The wind had stopped blowing.

Big John said to Tom, "Get your clothes."

Dinah packed Tom's clothes. She tied them in a small, neat roll.

She said, "I wish London weren't so far."

"It isn't so far," he said.

"When will you send for me?" she asked.

"As soon as I can," he said. "Don't forget, first we'll

have a room. Next we'll have a house. Then we'll have a garden."

She tried not to cry when they said good-by. Big John's wife stood beside her in the doorway. They both waved. Jacky looked out from behind them and made a face. Then Tom and Big John were on their way to London.

They walked through the village and down the road. Horses and wheels had made tracks in the snow. Tom and Big John walked in the tracks.

Late in the day they came to London. Tom had thought it would be a beautiful place. He was disappointed to find the streets so dirty. The smoke in the air made him sneeze.

But there was much to see. There were horses and carriages. There were Christmas trees in the windows. There were people everywhere—more people than Tom had ever seen before.

Big John took him to a room in an inn. It was a tiny room with a bed and a chair. There was a window that looked down on the street.

"Wait here," said Big John, "and don't try to go anywhere by yourself. If you do, you're sure to get lost."

He went away.

Tom looked out the window. The city was growing dark. He saw a lamplighter go by and light the lamps along the street.

Far away a church bell rang. He could hear boys and girls singing in the street. They were singing a Christmas song.

Tom turned from the window. He was sleepy and tired. He lay down on the bed and pulled the covers over him. Almost at once he was asleep.

There was a light in the room when he woke. Big John was there with a little man in a long black cloak.

"Get up." Big John pulled Tom out of bed. "You're going with Sparrow."

The other man had Tom's roll of clothing in his hands. He threw it, and Tom caught it.

"Come along, Redhead," he said.

Tom was still half asleep. Sparrow caught his arm and led him out of the room.

"Where are we going?" asked Tom.

"Not far," said the man.

"Isn't my uncle coming with us?"

"You don't see him, do you?"

They were out in the street. The cold air struck Tom in the face. He was wide awake now.

"Am I going to work for you?" he asked.

The man did not answer. He led the way down a dark street. Tom could smell the river. At the end of the street he could see light shining on the water.

They walked out onto a wharf. There was a plank from the wharf to the deck of a ship. Tom read the name on the ship. It was *Lady Peg.*

"Up you go," said Sparrow.

Tom drew back. "Why are we going on a ship?"

"Because I say so." The man pushed Tom up the plank.

"Wait!" said Tom. "I'll not go on this ship till you tell me—"

Sparrow gave him another push. Tom turned and began to fight.

"Leave off!" cried Sparrow. "You'll have us both in the water!"

"Get out of my way!" Tom struck Sparrow in the chest. The man slipped on the plank. He fell and pulled Tom down with him. Before Tom could get to his feet, he was caught in Sparrow's cloak.

He could not see or cry out. He could hardly breathe. Sparrow dragged him up the plank and onto the ship.

Tom heard a man ask, "Did he give you a fight?"

"That he did," said Sparrow. "My legs are black and blue."

"Take him below," said the other man. "Leave him in the crib till we're on our way."

4 · The Crib

The crib was a wooden cage below the deck of the ship. It was so small that when Tom stood up, his head came to the top. There was barely room for him to lie down.

It was dark all about him. He could see nothing, but he could hear footsteps above.

"Let me out!" he shouted. He beat on the crib. He kicked the door. "Let me out!"

Now and then he stopped to listen. No one answered him. He was not sure that anyone could hear him.

In the morning a little light came into the crib. Tom looked through the bars. He could see boxes and tubs and water barrels. He knew that he must be in the ship's storeroom.

There were footsteps on the deck above. Men were shouting. He felt the ship move.

A man came into the storeroom. He had brought a plate of food.

"Let me out!" said Tom.

"I can't be doing that," said the man. "I'm the cook on this ship, not the captain."

"I want to see the captain," said Tom.

"You'll be seeing him soon enough," said the cook.

"Why are they keeping me here?" asked Tom. "What's to be done with me?"

"You'll be knowing soon enough." The cook pushed the plate of food through the bars of the crib. He started away.

"Come back," said Tom.

"What now?" asked the cook.

"Won't you tell me whose ship this is and where it's taking us?" asked Tom.

"I can't stay and talk," said the man. "I've got my work." But he did stay a minute longer. "Eat your food. I put a bit of pudding on the side, because of Christmas."

Tom looked at the plate of salt fish with a bit of black pudding on the side. So it was Christmas Day, and this was his Christmas dinner.

5 · In the Cabin

The ship was two days at sea before Tom was let out of the crib.

It was Sparrow who opened the door.

"Keep quiet, and do as you're told," he said, "and you'll come to no harm."

He climbed a ladder and was gone.

Tom followed him up the ladder. He stepped out on deck. Some of the seamen turned to look at him, but no one spoke.

The cold wind nearly swept him off his feet. He looked out over the gray water. There was no land in sight.

He went to the other side of the deck where the wind was not so strong. A boy stood there by the rail. He was tall, with long arms and legs.

"You, there!" he said. "I never saw you before." He kept staring at Tom. "I was said to be the only boy on this ship. What might your name be?"

"Tom Pippin," Tom told him.

"Mine is Diggory—Diggory Smith," said the other boy. "Where did you come from? Did you drop down out of the sky?"

"I've been in the crib," said Tom.

"The crib? Oh, that's cruel!" said Diggory. "Why did they put you there?"

"I don't know," said Tom. "I know nothing of this ship or where it's sailing or why I'm on it."

"Then why did you come on board?" asked Diggory.

"I didn't *come* on board," said Tom. "A man *dragged* me. I tried to get away, and he threw me into the crib."

"I don't understand," said Diggory. "Start at the beginning. Tell me what happened."

Tom told him about coming to London with Big John. He told about Sparrow.

"Sparrow? I know him," said Diggory. "He's a seaman on this ship."

"He brought me here," said Tom.

"Now I see!" said Diggory. "Your uncle sold you."

"*Sold* me?" said Tom.

Diggory nodded. "He sold you to the captain of this ship. The captain sent Sparrow to bring you on board."

"No one could *sell* me!" said Tom.

"Ah, you know better than that," said Diggory. "You're bonded, Tom, the same as I am."

"Bonded?" said Tom.

"Captain Tooker paid your uncle to sign a paper," said Diggory. "It's a paper called a bond. The captain will take you across the sea to where workers are needed. He will sell your bond for as much money as he can get. Then you belong to the man who buys your bond, and you have to work for him."

"Like a slave?" asked Tom. "The rest of my life?"

"Oh, no," said Diggory. "Only seven years."

"Is this true," asked Tom, "or is it all just a story?"

"It's not a story. I know of such things," Diggory told him, "because my father bonded me to Captain Tooker. There were ten of us at home, with not enough to eat. I wished to go, and my brothers, too, but the captain would take only me. I was the only one old enough and strong enough." He said again, "I wished to go. This is my way of seeing the world. And after seven years I'll be free to make my fortune in America."

"America?" said Tom. "Is that where we're sailing?"

"Yes, for the islands of America," said Diggory.

"They've no right to send me there. They've no right to make a slave of me for seven years!" Tom asked, "Where is the captain?"

"In his cabin, I should think," said Diggory.

"Where is the cabin?" asked Tom.

Diggory pointed. "But don't you be going there. Captain Tooker is a hard man."

Tom was already on his way to the cabin.

He knocked at the door.

A voice called out, "Who's there?"

Tom opened the door. He stepped into a little room with wood walls and a soft, green rug. A man sat at a table. His face was small and rather mean, but he wore a fine brown wig, and the buttons on his coat were of gold.

"How dare you set foot in this cabin!" he shouted.

Tom stepped back.

"Stop!" cried the man. "Who are you?"

"Tom Pippin, sir," said Tom. "I wished to see the captain of the *Lady Peg*."

"Now that you've seen him, be on your way!"

"A word with you first, sir," said Tom. "Is it true that you bought my bond from my uncle?"

"Is it true?" said the captain. "Why else would you be here? Why else would I have you on my ship?"

"Then I have this to say," said Tom. "It was my uncle who signed the bond. It was not I. You may buy and sell me a hundred times, but I'll not be a slave to anyone!"

The captain's face was purple. He took a book from

the table and threw it. It caught Tom on the side of the head.

The captain took up a dish. Tom backed out of the cabin. He shut the door just as the dish broke against it.

Diggory was outside. He looked frightened.

"Quick, Tom!" he said.

They ran to the far end of the ship. Diggory pulled Tom down behind a pile of rope.

"It's a bad thing you've done," Diggory said in a whisper. "It's a bad, bad thing! Don't you know you're never to cross the captain? He's lord and master on this ship. Keep your head down. Stay out of his way till he's cooled off. If he finds you now, there's no telling what he might do."

"He hasn't any right—" began Tom.

"Don't you be talking that way," said Diggory. "He has every right, and you have none." He stopped. "That's blood on your face!"

"Yes," said Tom. "The captain threw a book—" He felt the ship roll beneath him. He closed his eyes. "I'm sick," he whispered.

6 · Diggory

For a week Tom lay ill. Some of the bonded men and women cared for him in the hold of the ship.

Two of Diggory's friends, Abel and Nancy, did the most to care for him. Abel was a young man from London. Nancy was his wife. Sometimes they scolded Tom, but always in a friendly way.

"You should never make the captain angry," said

Nancy. "It is well to be brave, but do not be foolish."

"The captain wished to have you beaten," said Abel. "I heard it from a sailor. But Sparrow told the captain, 'If we beat the boy, it may leave marks. Then he will not bring such a high price.'"

"You must keep out of the captain's way," said Nancy. "If he sees you, he may grow angry again. Stay in the hold. He never comes down here."

Before another week, Tom was strong again. The cut on his head was healed. But even after he was well, he stayed most of the time in the hold.

"It's an easy voyage," said Diggory. "There's bread and cheese enough for all, and the seamen do the work."

But the bonded people grew tired of the voyage. They grew tired of one another. There were quarrels in the hold.

Tom and Diggory stayed close to Abel and Nancy. There were no quarrels among them. Abel's head was full of stories he had heard, and he told them to Nancy and the boys.

He told of sea snakes that could swallow the biggest

ship in one mouthful. He told of pirates who sailed the seas, robbing ships along the way.

"Do you believe there are sea snakes?" asked Tom.

"It's only a story," said Abel, "but the pirates are real."

"I fear the pirates," said Nancy.

"We need not fear them," said Abel. "They care only for treasure."

"Then we are safe enough," said Nancy, "for indeed, this is no treasure ship."

Each day the *Lady Peg* sailed farther west and south. The winds were no longer cold. The sky was no longer gray and stormy.

There was a longboat on deck. Ropes and wooden blocks held it in place. Sometimes Tom left the hold and

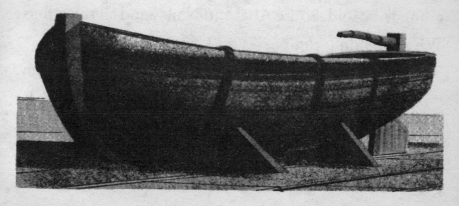

sat in the shadow of the longboat. Sometimes he and Diggory slept there at night.

One night they lay beside the longboat. They were both awake.

"What are you thinking of?" asked Diggory.

"My sister Dinah at home," said Tom. "What are you thinking of?"

"I'm thinking of America and what I'll do when I get there," said Diggory. "I wonder who will buy my bond. I hope my master will not be cruel and that I'll be strong enough to do his work. Tom, what if the same man buys us both? Then we can stay together."

"I won't be sold," said Tom.

"Why do you keep saying that?" asked Diggory. "I'm going to be sold. So are Abel and Nancy and all the others. Why shouldn't you be?"

"It's not the same for you and the others," said Tom. "You wanted to come on this ship. You chose to be bonded. I didn't choose. And I won't be sold."

"You can't help yourself," said Diggory. "When we get to America, men will come on board. They will look at us and bid for us. You will have to go with the man who bids highest for you."

"When we get on land, I'll run away," said Tom.

"You won't run far," said Diggory. "Do you know what they do when somebody runs away? They track him down with big dogs."

"I'm not afraid of their big dogs," said Tom.

"You'd better be afraid," said Diggory. "It's a cruel thing to be bonded against your will, but you *are* bonded. Why not make the best of it? It's only for seven years—"

"Seven years!" said Tom. "You talk as if that's nothing at all."

Diggory counted on his fingers. "In seven years you'll be nineteen. And I'll be twenty-two. That's not so old. Tom, promise me something."

"What?" asked Tom.

"Promise me you'll do nothing to get yourself in trouble. Promise me you'll think no more of getting away."

Tom only lay there, looking up at the stars. He would not promise.

7 · *Sail Ho!*

At sunrise the next morning a shout awakened them: "Sail ho!"

"A ship!" said Diggory. "That means there's a ship in sight."

He and Tom ran to the rail.

Diggory asked a seaman, "Which way is the ship?"

"That way." The man pointed. "Can you see her?"

"Yes," said Diggory.

Tom went back to the shadow of the longboat. Captain Tooker had come on deck.

The captain stood by the rail, with a spyglass to his eye. It was a long time before he went back to his cabin.

Tom went to the rail again. The ship had come nearer. Her white sails hardly showed against the clouds.

Most of the bonded people had come up from the hold. They were watching the ship.

Abel and Nancy stood with Tom and Diggory.

"Is she an English ship?" asked Nancy.

"She may be French," said Abel.

"Or Spanish," said someone else.

The ship was faster than the *Lady Peg*. By late afternoon she had come so near that they could see men on her deck.

She flew no flag. She did not answer the captain's shouts and signals.

Captain Tooker said in anger, "She shall come no closer until we know what flag she flies." He called out, "Man the cannon!"

Seamen sprang to the row of cannon along the rail.

"When I give the word," said Captain Tooker, "fire a shot to warn the ship away."

The ship came nearer.

"Fire!" said the captain.

One of the gunners put a match to his cannon. The cannon roared.

The shot was meant to fall in the path of the ship. But the gunner's aim was poor. The cannon ball struck the deck of the ship and tore away part of the rail.

The ship fired back. Smoke and flame shot from her cannon.

Diggory cried out, "She's running up her flag!"

Tom held his breath as the flag went up. It was the black flag of a pirate ship.

A woman began to scream.

Cannon balls struck the water beside the *Lady Peg*.

Someone shouted, "Keep your heads down!"

The bonded men and women were running for the hold. Tom and Diggory were carried along with them. Down the stairs they went, half-climbing, half-falling.

They drew close together in the hold.

"We should not have run away," said Abel. "We should go help fight."

"No, no!" Nancy caught his arm. "I'll not let you go!"

"This is not our fight," said another of the men. "We mean no more than sheep to Captain Tooker. Let *him* fight the pirates."

The hold shook, as if something had run against the ship.

"Hark!" said Abel. "They're alongside us now."

There was a rush of steps overhead. There were pistol shots.

Then all was quiet on deck.

In the hold all was quiet, too. Everyone listened. Everyone was waiting.

A voice called down the stairway, "Come out, one at a time. Come quietly, and you'll not be harmed."

Nancy held to Abel's hand. "What shall we do?"

"We'll do as he says," answered Abel. "There's nothing else left for us."

He helped her up the stairs. The others followed them.

8 · Captain Land

Tom stepped out on deck into a circle of pirates. There were young and old among them. Most of them wore silk and velvet in black, white, and the brightest of reds and blues. Some had pistols ready, some had knives.

The pirate captain was young. His face was thin and dark. He spoke like an English gentleman.

"Put down your weapons," he said. "All your knives

37

and swords and pistols—put them here on the deck."

"We have no weapons," said Abel. "We are only poor bonded people."

One of the women cried out, "Spare us, good captain!"

"Your lives will be spared," said the pirate captain. "Your Captain Tooker was wise enough to end a fight he could not win. Because of that, he and his men will be spared. But he was a fool to fire on me. For this he must pay."

Two of the pirates went to the captain's cabin. They led out Captain Tooker and his men. Captain Tooker tried to walk bravely, but his legs shook with fear.

"Make the longboat ready," said the pirate captain.

"The longboat? Do you mean to put us out to sea?" Captain Tooker's face was pale. "We shall be lost!"

"There are islands near. You have sails in the boat, and you have oars," said the pirate captain.

"But my ship—!" cried Captain Tooker.

"The ship is yours no longer," said the pirate captain. "Be quick. You waste my time."

Captain Tooker's men let the longboat down.

"The bonded people will be first to leave the ship," said the pirate captain.

Men and women began to go over the side. They climbed down a rope ladder and into the boat.

Tom and Diggory stood together.

"It's your turn," said Diggory.

Tom did not move.

Diggory gave him a push toward the rope ladder.

Tom turned. He started across the deck.

A pirate stopped him. He was a tall black man with gold rings in his ears.

"Let me speak to your captain," said Tom.

"Captain! Captain Land!" called the black man. "The boy would speak to you."

The pirate captain stood nearby. "Speak," he said.

"Take me with you," said Tom.

Captain Land looked down at him. "What is this?"

"They stole me away from London. They had no right to bond me," said Tom. "Take me with you."

Captain Tooker was listening. "Hear the young dog!" he cried.

"Silence!" said the pirate captain. "The boy speaks bravely, and go with me he shall!"

Diggory gave Tom a frightened look before he went over the side.

Captain Tooker and his men climbed into the longboat.

The longboat cast off. Some of the seamen rowed. Others worked to put up the sail.

Captain Land looked about him. "So this is the *Lady Peg*. *Lady Pig* would be a better name. A pigboat it is, fit for nothing but to burn! Follow me," he said to Tom.

The pirate ship lay alongside the *Lady Peg*. Captain Land jumped down onto the deck of his ship. Tom jumped after him.

The crew was busy looting the *Lady Peg*. Some of the men had their arms full of clothing. Others had the chairs and the green rug from Captain Tooker's cabin.

"There's little enough that's worth taking," said one of the men.

"A pigboat, that's what it is," said another.

The pirates carried the loot to their ship. The last

one to leave the *Lady Peg* threw lighted torches behind him.

The men loosed the hooks and ropes that held the ships together. The pirate ship moved away.

Night had fallen. Tom stood beside Captain Land and watched the *Lady Peg* burn.

The fire burned slowly until it came to the room where the gunpowder was kept. Then there was a great explosion. The ship broke in two. Sparks and flame leaped high into the air and lighted the sea for miles around.

9 · The Pirate Ship

Tom slept that night in Captain Land's cabin. His bed was a hammock.

When he woke, he saw the captain having breakfast. There was a teapot on the table. There were oranges and biscuits in silver dishes. The captain was eating biscuits dipped in tea.

Tom moved in the hammock.

The captain asked, "Are you awake?"

"Yes, sir," said Tom.

"You were crying out in your sleep," said the captain. "What were you dreaming?"

"I don't know, sir," said Tom.

"Once you said 'Diggory.' Who is Diggory?"

"He was my friend on Captain Tooker's ship," said Tom.

"Have no fear for Diggory. The sea is not rough. The longboat will reach shore," said the captain. "What is your name, boy? Tom Pippin—that's it. Pull up a chair, Tom Pippin, if you want a bite of breakfast."

Tom sat down at the table. He drank a cup of tea and ate a biscuit. He looked at the oranges.

"Would you like one?" asked the captain.

"Yes, if it please you," said Tom.

"Then take it."

Tom took an orange.

"Have you ever had an orange before?" asked the captain.

"Yes, sir," said Tom. "Always at Christmas my father brought some home."

"Was it your father who bonded you?"

"It was my uncle," said Tom.

"And you have no wish to be bonded?" said Captain Land. "You would rather be a pirate."

"A pirate?" said Tom. "*No, sir!*"

The captain gave him a long look. "You *don't* wish to be a pirate?"

"No, sir," said Tom.

"Then why did you choose to come with me?"

"I wished to be free," said Tom. "I thought you might put me ashore somewhere. Then I could find a ship back to England."

"Your uncle would only bond you again," said the captain.

"I would not tell him where I was," said Tom, "but I would let my sister know. She is waiting for me."

"Ah," said Captain Land. Then he was quiet for a while.

They finished breakfast. They went out on deck.

Some of the men came close for a look at Tom.

"He's a redhead for sure!" one of them said.

Tom listened to them talk. He learned that the name of the pirate ship was the *Sea Bird*. He began to learn the names of the men.

The little man with the cruel face and long arms was called Spider. The black man was Benjy. There was a man named Duke, who was talking, laughing, or singing most of the time.

Duke said to Captain Land, "What shall we do with this redheaded pirate? Can he fire a pistol or throw a knife? Shall I teach him what he will need to know?"

"Teach him nothing," said the captain. "The boy is not a pirate, and he has no wish to be."

After sundown Tom sat on deck. He watched the waves. He heard the wind sing as it filled the sails.

Benjy the black man sat down near him. "You like the ship?" he asked in his soft, deep voice. "You like the sea?"

"Yes," said Tom.

"I, too," said Benjy. Once he had been a slave, he told Tom. His master was kind to him and taught him many

things. "Then he died, and I was sold again," said Benjy. "My new master was a bad man. Captain Land saved me from him. Now Captain Land is my master. I follow him everywhere."

"Will you tell me something?" asked Tom.

"If I can," said Benjy.

"Where are we now?"

"In the waters of America," said Benjy. "To the west

lie the Florida islands. To the south lies the great island of Cuba. Have you heard of them?"

"I've seen them on a map," said Tom. "Where are we going now? To Florida?"

"No," said Benjy. "We go to careen the ship."

" 'Careen the ship'? What does that mean?" asked Tom.

"It means we clean the ship," said Benjy. "We run close to shore and turn the ship on her side. We scrape away the sea plants and the little shellfish. They hold fast to the wood. We must scrape them away before they grow hard and heavy like stone."

"Where will you go to careen the ship?" asked Tom.

"To our island," said Benjy.

"What island is that?" asked Tom.

"The island of the pirates," said Benjy. "It is where the pirates go to careen their ships. They stop there for food and water. They rest there after a long voyage. It is where they are safe from the law." He smiled at Tom. "It is our own island. You will see it tomorrow."

10 · The Island

In the morning Tom saw the island. There was a beach of shining white sand. Beyond the beach was a bright green jungle. Birds flew in and out of the jungle and over the boats in the harbor. It was a beautiful sight.

But the town on the harbor was far from beautiful. It was a town of huts and tents. The huts were made of driftwood and palm leaves. The tents were made of old sails that flapped in the wind. There were broken bottles in the streets.

Tom went ashore with Benjy and Captain Land. Benjy carried a hammock, a water bottle, and the captain's sea chest.

There were ragged, barefoot people on the wharf. Most of them were men, but a few were women and children.

"These people live here," Benjy told Tom. "They hunt and fish and have gardens. On this island they can live without much work."

"Where did they come from?" asked Tom.

"Many places," said Benjy. "Some were shipwrecked here. Some came to be safe from the law."

"Why doesn't the law come here?" asked Tom.

Benjy told him, "Near our island the sea is not deep, and our ships are small and light. We can sail these waters. But the ships of the law are not small and light. They would be wrecked here."

Captain Land led the way past the town and down the beach.

At the edge of the jungle they came to a small house. Vines had grown over it until it was almost hidden.

"It is the captain's house. He sleeps here when we are on the island," said Benjy. "It is good and strong, this house. I made it myself from an old wrecked ship."

The door was open. Tom looked inside. There was only one room, and it was empty.

Benjy told Tom and the captain, "Do not go inside yet. There may be snakes or spiders with poison in their bites."

He went into the house. With a palm branch he swept the walls and floor. He put up the hammock and set the sea chest beside it.

Afterward Tom went with him to find food and water. They went to a clearing in the jungle. There was a well in the clearing.

Benjy took the cover off the well. He let down the bottle and drew it up full of water.

Near the well Tom found a vine heavy with grapes.

"Pick some for our captain," said Benjy, "while I find something more."

He took the pistol out of his belt. He went on into the jungle.

Tom put two leaves together to make a basket. He filled it with grapes. Then he sat down on the well cover to wait for Benjy.

He thought of his sister, Dinah. He wondered how long it would be before they were together again. How surprised she would be, he thought, if she could see him here in this island jungle!

In a little while Benjy was back. He had shot a young goat. He carried it over his shoulder. Tom carried the water and the grapes.

As they came out of the jungle, someone called, "Halloo!"

They stopped and looked back.

Three men were sitting on the beach. There was a cook-fire near them on the sand. Over the fire hung part of a roasted pig.

One of the men was picking his teeth with a long knife.

He called again, "Halloo! Boy! Come here!"

Tom went to where the men were sitting. The man who had called him wore velvet and lace and fine leather

boots. He wore a hat with purple feathers. A thick, red
beard covered half his face.

"Now here is a sight I never thought to see," he said.

"Here is a lad with hair as red as my beard! Where do you come from, boy?"

"From England, sir," said Tom.

"Where do you go with your grapes and water bottle?"

"To the house of Captain Land," answered Tom.

The man sat up straight. "Is Captain Land your master?"

"I am my own master," said Tom.

The man burst out laughing. "You are not afraid to speak up, I see. No more was I afraid when I was young. Good day, lad. Get along with you. We may meet again."

Tom and Benjy went away.

Benjy said, "You must not be so bold."

"Did I say something wrong?" asked Tom.

Benjy did not answer. He said nothing more until they were back at the house.

Captain Land was lying in the hammock. Benjy told him, "Captain Red is here."

"Ah," said Captain Land, and a strange look came into his eyes.

11 · Captain Red

That night the crew of the *Sea Bird* camped along the beach. The next day they were ready to clean the ship. They ran her close to shore. With ropes they pulled her over on her side and tied her to a tree that grew near the water.

Captain Land kept to his house. He had a fever, he said.

Benjy told Tom, "It is island fever. Always it comes to him here. But he is soon well again."

Benjy and Tom took turns staying with Captain Land. Sometimes, when Benjy was at the house, Tom walked along the beach by himself.

He found a little bay where waves came up over the rocks. It was hidden from the rest of the beach by sand hills. He liked to sit there and look out to sea.

One day a man came upon him in the little bay. It was the man with the red beard.

"Halloo!" he called. "Why are you hiding there?"

"I am *not* hiding," answered Tom.

"It would do you no good if you were. Anyone could see your red head a mile away." The man came down over the sand hills. "I want a word with you, English boy. How did you come to this island?"

"I came with Captain Land," said Tom.

"What brought you and Captain Land together?"

"I was on an English ship," said Tom. "I was bonded against my will. Captain Land kept me from being sold."

"And now you are your own master," said the man.

"Yes, sir," said Tom.

"Then you shall sail with me," said the man. "There is my ship across the harbor. I sail tomorrow." He began to laugh. "What a pair we will make — I with my red beard, you with your red head!"

"Are you not a — a pirate?" asked Tom.

"That I am, and one of the best," said the man. "Captain Red, they call me. It is a name men know and fear around the world. Do you want adventure, English boy? I'll show you adventure. Do you want gold? You'll see more gold than you can count, and maybe some of it for you. Speak up, English boy. Has the cat got your tongue?"

"I was only thinking," said Tom. "Adventure and gold may be very well, but not — not the rest of it."

"Not the rest of it?" Captain Red frowned. "What do you mean?"

"Not the life of a pirate," said Tom.

"Why, it's the best life there is!" cried Captain Red.

"Not for me," said Tom.

"You're a strange one. You wouldn't be bonded. The

life of a pirate is not good enough for you," said Captain
Red. "What *do* you want?"

"I want to go back to England," said Tom. "My sister
is there. I want to work and make a home so that we
can be together."

Captain Red asked, "How will you get back to England?"

"Captain Land will help me," said Tom. "He will put me ashore where I can find a ship to take me back."

"He cannot sail until his ship is ready," said Captain Red, "and that will not be soon. I passed by the *Sea Bird* an hour ago, and no man was working. They were all in town or sleeping in the shade. But my ship sails tomorrow. You shall sail with me, English boy."

"Captain Land will help me find a way back to England," Tom told him. "He has said so."

"And so do I," said Captain Red. "Do you think I would turn a boy into a pirate against his will? One week from today I'll have you on a ship to England. Is that good enough for you?"

"Yes, sir!" said Tom. "I thank you kindly."

"I want no thanks," said Captain Red. "Come. We'll go to my ship."

"First I must see Captain Land," said Tom.

"Why?" asked Captain Red.

"I must say good-by," said Tom.

Already he was on his way, running across the beach toward Captain Land's house.

12 · A Boy in Carolina

Benjy had built a small fire in front of the house. There was a kettle on the fire, and he was bending over it. He smiled when Tom came running up.

"The medicine I make is good," said Benjy. "Today our captain is nearly well."

"Is he inside?" asked Tom. "I want to say good-by."

Benjy stopped smiling. "Good-by?"

"A ship is sailing from here tomorrow," said Tom.

"The captain is going to put me ashore where I can–"

Benjy asked quickly, "What captain?"

"Captain Red," answered Tom.

"No, no!" cried Benjy. "You will not go with Captain Red!"

"But why?" asked Tom.

"He is bad," said Benjy. "You would not believe how bad he is."

"He is a pirate, I know," said Tom, "but he promised to help me find a ship back to England."

"You must not trust him," said Benjy. "Do you know why he is here now? He was in a battle at sea. Many of his men were killed or wounded. He is here to find men to take their places. His cabin boy was killed. If you sail with him, you will never go back to England. You will be the cabin boy of Captain Red."

"Why should he want *me* for his cabin boy?" asked Tom.

"I do not know," said Benjy. "It may please him that your hair is the color of his beard. Or he may wish to make our captain angry by taking you away. He has long been an enemy of our captain. Surely you knew that."

"How could I know it?" said Tom. "No one told me."

"Our captain once took a prize from under Captain Red's very nose," said Benjy. "The prize was a Spanish ship that carried gold and silver. Captain Red will never forget."

Captain Land had come to the doorway. He called Tom into the house.

"It's time I talked to you," he said. "All that Benjy has told you is true. Captain Red is a friend to no one. He is cruel. He does not keep his word. I am a pirate, yet I can speak the truth. Do you believe me?"

"Yes, sir," said Tom.

"Listen," said Captain Land. "I'll tell you a story."

The story was about a boy in America. He was born near the city of Charlestown in a place called Carolina. His name was Davy Tanner.

His home was a plantation where rice and sugar cane were grown. His mother and father were good to him. They gave him a pony cart and a pony. They sent him to England where he lived with his uncle and went to school.

When Davy came home he was a man. "Now I need you here," said his father. "I need you to help me on the plantation."

But Davy was not ready to stay. He wanted to see more of the world. He and his father quarreled, and Davy left home.

He fell in with a band of pirates. Their ship was wrecked off the Carolina shore. They were caught and thrown into prison.

Some other pirates broke into the prison and set him free. He ran away to sea with them.

But he missed the plantation. He missed his mother and father.

One night he went back. His father would not open the door.

"You are a pirate now. You have brought shame upon us," said his father. "Leave this plantation and never come back. I shall try to forget I ever had a son!"

Davy went back to his ship. He took another name,

so that he would bring no more shame to his father and mother. Time went by, and he became captain of a pirate ship.

But he was weary of the sea. He was weary of a pirate's life.

He could not go home again. He could not go ashore and live the life of an honest man. Too many people knew his face. He would be sent to prison or put to death.

That was the end of Captain Land's story.

He asked Tom, "Do you know the man in my story? Do you know his name?"

"Is it—Captain Land?" asked Tom.

"Yes," said the captain. "I know this life, and I'll not let you be drawn into it. Trust me, and I'll look after you."

They heard Benjy's voice outside, "Why do you come here?"

Someone else spoke in a loud voice, "English boy! Come out! I am waiting!"

It was Captain Red.

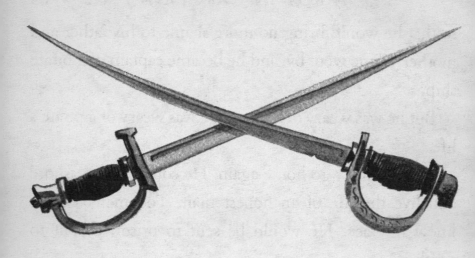

13 · The Meeting

Captain Land opened the door.

Captain Red took off his hat and made a mock bow. "Good day to you. Where is the boy?"

"The boy is here," said Captain Land.

"I've come for him," said Captain Red.

"The boy is here," said Captain Land, "and here he stays."

"English boy!" called Captain Red. "I'll have a word with you."

Tom went to the door.

"Are you ready?" asked Captain Red. "Shall we go?"

"No, sir," said Tom. "I—I'll stay with Captain Land."

"This is strange," said Captain Red. "Half an hour ago you were ready to go with me. What changed your mind?"

"I changed his mind," said Captain Land. "I told him you were a friend to no one. I told him your word was not to be trusted. And there's much more I might have said."

"You've hated me always," said Captain Red.

"And you have hated me," said Captain Land.

"That I have," said Captain Red. "I hate you all day, and I wake up at night hating you!"

He took a step forward. With his open hand, he struck Captain Land in the face.

Captain Land stood still for a moment. Then he spoke in a quiet voice, "When shall we meet?"

"Whenever you say," said Captain Red.

"Tonight?" said Captain Land. "When the moon rises?"

"Good," said Captain Red. "And where?"

"On the beach," said Captain Land, "by the old fort?"

Captain Red nodded. "Swords or pistols?" he asked.

"Swords," said Captain Land.

Captain Red showed his teeth in a smile. "Until tonight," he said, and he walked away.

Benjy had been listening. "Master!" he cried. "You must not!"

Captain Land looked at the fire Benjy had made. It was almost out.

"Build up your fire and make my medicine," he said. "I need to be strong tonight."

He went back into the house.

Tom brought wood for the fire. He asked Benjy, "What did they mean? Are they going to fight?"

"Yes," said Benjy.

"Is it because of me?" asked Tom.

"Do not blame yourself," said Benjy. "The fight has been a long time in the making."

The new wood caught fire. The kettle began to boil. Benjy put in more leaves and bark. Tom heard him whisper, "Medicine, be strong!"

14 · In the Moonlight

As the day went by, Benjy said over and over, "Do not fight, Captain. You are not yet well and strong. Do not fight tonight."

At last the captain told him to be quiet. "I am well enough and strong enough," he said.

"Then call the crew and let us fight beside you," said Benjy. "Call them together, and we will all fight Captain Red and his men."

"No," said Captain Land. "This is between Captain Red and myself."

Night came, and the moon rose. The captain buckled on his sword.

"If you must fight," said Benjy, "may I be with you?"

"Yes," said Captain Land, "but no one else."

He and Benjy went away.

Tom sat alone. The house was warm. Bugs and moths were flying about the candle flame.

He went outside.

The beach was white in the moonlight. He could see the tracks Captain Land and Benjy had made in the sand.

He tried not to think about the fight. Birds were crying in the jungle. The sounds they made were lonesome and strange. He tried not to hear them.

He went back into the house.

It seemed a long time before he heard footsteps outside. He opened the door a little way. He saw Benjy's face in the moonlight, and he opened the door wide.

Benjy came into the house. He carried Captain Land in his arms.

The captain's eyes were closed. The front of his shirt was wet with blood.

Benjy put him down in the hammock.

The captain's eyes opened. He tried to lift his head.

Benjy knelt beside him. With a knife he began to cut away the cloth from the wound.

"Stop," said the captain.

"Do not try to talk," said Benjy.

"I must," said Captain Land. "Listen to me. Take the gold pieces, Benjy. Take the gold pieces in my sea chest. They are yours. . . . Tom?"

Tom went close to him.

"I lost the fight. I was too slow." The captain coughed. He closed his eyes for a moment. "Go to Charlestown. Go to my people. They will help you."

His voice had become a whisper. He turned his face away.

Benjy laid his hand over the captain's heart.

"Captain—!"

He put his head down against the hammock and began to weep. "Master, master!" he cried.

Tom was weeping, too.

He heard someone at the door, but he did not turn. He did not look up until the door opened.

Captain Red stood in the doorway. One of his men was with him. The two came into the house.

They looked down on the face of Captain Land. Then they looked at each other. Captain Red nodded and laughed.

"Come, English boy," he said.

Before Tom knew how it had happened, he was outside, walking with Captain Red.

"I must go back," he said.

"You will do as I say, English boy," said Captain Red. "You will come with me."

He and the other man took Tom by the arms.

Tom walked between them. He saw the lights of town ahead. He saw the lights of Captain Red's ship in the harbor.

He tried to think of a way to escape. Once he was aboard the ship, he might *never* escape.

Captain Red seemed to know what he was thinking.

He held Tom's arm more tightly. Near the edge of town, he looked back. Tom looked back, too.

Like a shadow, someone had come up behind them. It was Benjy.

He threw himself at Captain Red. He swung his fist like a hammer. The captain fell.

The other man had drawn his pistol. Tom caught his arm. The man fired into the sand. As he fought to throw Tom off, Benjy struck him down.

"Run!" said Benjy.

Tom ran. Benjy was beside him. They ran through the bright moonlight, across the beach and into the jungle.

15 · A Strange Journey

It was dark among the trees. Tom and Benjy felt their way. They stayed close together so they would not be lost from each other.

They walked until Tom was tired. He could not keep up with Benjy's long steps.

Benjy stopped. "Rest now," he said.

"Will they look for us?" asked Tom.

"Yes," said Benjy, "but they will not find us here tonight."

They lay down in the wet jungle grass. Toward morning Tom went to sleep.

It was daylight when he woke. Benjy was there with fruit and nuts that he had found. Tom ate a little. Benjy ate nothing.

Tom looked up at the trees that shut out the sun. "No one could find us here," he said.

"Yes," said Benjy. "If we stay on this island very long, Captain Red and his men will find us. They will hunt us down."

They started on through the jungle.

They walked until they came to the sea. They had come all the way across the island.

Benjy found a hiding place for Tom. It was in the branches of a tree. "Do not show yourself until I call," he said.

Tom sat in the tree. Through the leaves he could see the sky. He watched it grow dark. The stars were out when he heard Benjy call softly from below.

Tom climbed down.

"Do not talk," said Benjy in a whisper.

With hardly a sound, they walked to the beach. A boat lay at the edge of the water.

Tom got into the boat. Benjy pushed it into the water. He got in and took the oars.

They were a long way from shore before he spoke. "Our luck held good. There was no one to see us go."

The boat smelled of fish and seaweed.

"Where did you get this boat?" asked Tom.

"I took it from a fisherman," answered Benjy. "I fought him for it."

"Where are we going?" asked Tom.

"Far from here," said Benjy.

He set up a sail, and it caught the wind. The little boat sailed out to sea.

It was the beginning of a strange journey. For days and weeks the boat sailed along a chain of islands. Some of the islands were green with trees. Others were no more than bare rocks.

On one of the islands Benjy killed a young goat. He cut the goat meat into strips and hung them over a fire. When they were smoked and dry they were good to eat.

He and Tom ate the smoked meat while they sailed from island to island.

They had fish to eat, too, and turtles and turtles' eggs. There was always food in the boat, yet day by day Benjy grew thinner. He never smiled. Tom never saw him sleep.

Once Tom woke and found him weeping. They were sailing by moonlight. Benjy was steering the boat with an oar. Tears shone on his face.

"What is it, Benjy?" asked Tom.

"I think of my master," said Benjy. "I weep for him."

One day they landed on an island.

"There is a harbor not far away," said Benjy. "There is a city on the harbor."

"Do you know this island?" asked Tom.

"I knew it once," said Benjy.

He cut four poles and set them up on the beach. He turned the boat upside down and Tom helped him set it on top of the poles. The boat was the roof of their house. They stuck sticks in the sand to make the walls.

Benjy went to the city on the harbor. He brought back a suit of clothes for Tom. He brought a shirt, shoes, and stockings, too.

"Try them," he said.

"Where did you find these clothes?" asked Tom.

"I bought them," said Benjy.

"How did you pay for them?" asked Tom.

"With gold that our captain left to me," said Benjy.

Tom took off his ragged clothes. He tried on the new ones. They fit very well.

"Now," said Benjy, "you will be ready."

Every day he went to the harbor. He watched the ships come and go.

The day came when he ran all the way back from town.

"Make ready," he said. "There is a ship in the harbor that will sail soon for Charlestown in Carolina."

Tom went with Benjy to town.

Benjy pointed to the ship at the dock. "Go on board. Tell the captain where you wish to go. Tell him you can pay."

"I cannot pay," said Tom.

"Yes," said Benjy. He put two gold pieces into Tom's hand.

"Aren't you coming with me?" asked Tom.

"That could not be," said Benjy. "But I have kept my promise."

"What promise?" asked Tom.

"My master wished you to go to Charlestown," said Benjy. "In my heart I promised him I would help you find a way."

Tom went on board the ship. He found the captain. He asked, "Will you take me to Charlestown?"

"Can you pay?" asked the captain.

Tom showed him one of the gold pieces.

"It is not enough," said the captain.

Tom showed him the other gold piece.

The captain nodded. "I will take you there."

Tom went to the rail. He looked for Benjy. He wanted to say good-by. But Benjy was gone.

16 · The Plantation House

The voyage to Carolina was smooth, with fair skies and good winds. Only a few days after he had boarded ship, Tom was in Charlestown.

The city looked clean and new. Its harbor was a busy place.

Tom spoke to some men on the dock. He asked them the way to the Tanner plantation.

"Take the river road," one of them told him, "until

you come to a white house with trees all around it. Can you read?"

"Yes, sir," said Tom.

"Then you'll see the name on the gate," said the man.

Tom took the river road to the Tanner plantation. He knocked at the door of the tall white house.

A maid looked out at him.

He told her his name. "May I see Master Tanner, please?"

The maid showed him into a large, quiet room. A man was there, writing at a desk. A woman sat near him.

The man's hair was gray. He had a thin, handsome face. He looked up from the desk.

Tom bowed. "Good day, sir. I–" He stopped. He did not know how to go on.

"Have you nothing to say?" asked the man.

"Yes, sir," said Tom. "It is about your son."

The woman cried out, then put her hand to her mouth.

Master Tanner said, "My son has brought shame to this house. His name is not spoken here."

"But let me tell you—" Tom began.

Master Tanner stood up. "I'll hear no more. You may go."

Tom bowed and went quickly away. He started down the hall.

Someone called, "Wait!"

The woman was running after him.

"Tell me," she said, "have you seen my son? Is he well? Did he send you here?"

"He wished me to come here," said Tom. "It was the last thing he told me."

"Where is he?" she asked. "What word do you have?"

"It is word I am sorry to bring," said Tom.

She had been watching his face. She said, "I think I know. My son is dead."

He nodded.

She turned her head. With her handkerchief to her eyes, she left him.

When she came back, Master Tanner was with her. He looked tired and old.

"I did not know." He took Tom's hand. "I thank you for coming here. Will you come and sit with Mistress Tanner and me?"

Tom sat with them. Mistress Tanner began to talk of her son.

"How did you meet him?" she asked.

Tom told the story. The room grew dark while he talked. The maid came in to light the candles.

"I have talked too long, and now it is late," said Tom. "I must start back to Charlestown."

"Not tonight," said Master Tanner.

"No," said Mistress Tanner. "You must stay with us tonight."

17 · The Moon and a Garden

Tom said the next morning, "I must go to Charlestown to see what ships are there."

"I have already sent a servant," said Master Tanner. "He will bring us word of any ships that sail to England."

"You must stay a while with us," said Mistress Tanner. "We will show you where our son played when he was a boy."

The days passed quickly. Tom walked in the plantation fields and woods. He swam in the river. He rode in the Tanner carriage.

One day word came from Charlestown. An English ship was in port. She would soon be sailing for home.

"I have no money," said Tom, "but I can work on the ship."

Master Tanner went to Charlestown to see what might be done.

In the evening he came home. He found Tom reading in the library. "I spoke with the ship's captain," said Master Tanner. "He has no place for you."

"Not even if I work?" asked Tom.

"No, but you can send a letter on the ship."

"I'll write to Dinah!" said Tom. "I'll tell her not to worry and I'll surely be home on the next ship."

"You need not go," said Master Tanner.

"What did you say, sir?" asked Tom.

"We have been glad to have you here—Mistress Tanner and I," said Master Tanner. "We like to see you about the plantation. It almost seems we have a son again.

You need not go back to England. There is much I could do for you here. When you are a little older, there is much you could do to help me."

"I thank you, sir," said Tom. "I thank you ever so much, but I must go back. My sister is waiting."

"Would she be happy here?" asked Master Tanner. "My brother lives near London. If I ask him to, he will seek out your sister and place her on a ship to America. I can send him a letter tomorrow. You can send your sister a letter so that she may be ready."

Tom sat very still. He did not know what to say.

"I have spoken too quickly," said Master Tanner. "Think about it now. Come to me when your mind is made up."

He left Tom alone in the library.

Tom thought of Dinah. The journey to America was long. Would she be afraid to come so far?

But many others had made the journey—some of them no older than Dinah.

Would she be happy here?

He looked out into the night. Through the window

he saw the garden with its walks and flowers and trees. Above it was the moon.

He thought of Dinah's wish: a place where they could be together—a garden where she could watch the moon come up....

All at once he knew. She *would* be happy here. And so would he.

IMMANUEL LUTHERAN SCHOOL
SCHOEN MEMORIAL LIBRARY